LITTLE TROLL

Collins
YELLOW
STORYBOOK

Other Collins Yellow Storybooks

LiTTLE TROLL

ALAN DURANT

ILLUSTRATED BY JULEK HELLER

Collins
An imprint of HarperCollins*Publishers*

First published in Great Britain by Collins in 1998
Collins is an imprint of HarperCollins*Publishers* Ltd
77-85 Fulham Palace Road, Hammersmith, London, W6 8JB

3 5 7 9 8 6 4

Text copyright © Alan Durant 1998
Illustrations copyright © Julek Heller 1998

ISBN 0 00 675375 2

Printed and bound in Great Britain by
Omnia Books Ltd. Glasgow.

CONTENTS

Little Troll and the Monster

Little Troll was cross. He didn't know why exactly, he just was.

"You must have got out of the
wrong side of bed," said his mum.

But Little Troll hadn't. He was
cross when he woke up.

"You look like you've been eating sour plums for breakfast," said his dad.

But Little Troll hadn't. He had eaten his favourite cereal for breakfast, but he was still cross.

On his way to school, Little Troll muttered rude words to himself. "Yuk sucks banana pooh," said Little Troll. He got more and more cross.

Then he met a monster.

"Where are you going?" asked the monster.

"To school," said Little Troll crossly.

"I'll come with you," said the monster.

So Little Troll went to school, and so did the monster.

The monster followed Little
Troll into the playground. All the
pupils were there, playing happily.

Little Troll saw his friends —
Sprite and Goblin and Faun and
Elf. They were playing tag.

Little Troll watched them and the monster watched too.

"Come and play, Little Troll," cried his friends.

But Little Troll scowled and shook his head. The monster scowled and shook his head too.

The bell rang and the pupils ran into class. Little Troll and the monster went in last.

Everyone in Little Troll's class had someone to sit next to. Except Little Troll.

Little Troll sat down at the back of the room. The monster sat next to him.

"Good morning, class," said Miss Witherkins.

"Good morning, Miss Witherkins," said the class.

Miss Witherkins called the register. When she called Little Troll's name, he grunted.

"Please don't grunt, Little Troll," said Miss Witherkins. "Speak nicely."

The monster chewed a pencil,
which he did not like, and
swallowed an eraser, which he did.
Then he ate some paper.

"Yum," he said.

"Right, we'll start with maths," said Miss Witherkins. She handed out some maths books.

The monster nibbled the corner of one page. Then he ate the whole book. He ate adding-up sums and taking-away sums. He ate times tables.

The monster burped loudly.
So did Little Troll.

"Little Troll!" said Miss
Witherkins. "That is very rude! I
think you'd better come and sit at
this empty desk at the front where I
can see you."

So Little Troll sat at the front by the teacher and the monster went too.

Then the monster got bored. He turned around and he rolled his monster eyes, and he waggled his monster ears. Then he stuck out his monster tongue.

So did Little Troll.

"Little Troll!" said Miss
Witherkins. "That is very, very
rude! I think you'd better go and
stand in the corner of the room."

So Little Troll stood in the
corner and the monster went too.

But the monster could not stand still. First he stood on one monster leg and then on the other.

He stood on his head. Then he put his head between his legs and pulled a monstrous face. Then he giggled.

So did Little Troll.

"Little Troll!" said Miss
Witherkins. "I have had enough.
You'd better go and see Mrs Mab
and tell her what you find so
funny." Mrs Mab was the head
teacher and she could be
very scary.

Little Troll and the monster
walked to Mrs Mab's room.

Little Troll thought cross
thoughts. "I'm not scared of Mrs
Mab," he thought.

"Nor am I," said the monster.

The monster walked into Mrs Mab's room and ate her in one monster mouthful.
He ate her desk too.

The monster went back to the classroom with Little Troll and ate Miss Witherkins.
Then he ate her desk and her chair.

He ate the chalk and the chalkboard and the board duster.

The monster ate all the books and the pencils and the pens and the paintbrushes.

He ate a pile of empty egg boxes and a toilet roll.

He ate a beautiful model castle that the class had made.

Then he started to eat the pupils. He ate Sprite and Elf and Faun and Goblin.

He ate everyone and everything, until there was no one left but Little Troll.

Little Troll started to cry.

Mrs Mab opened her door and saw Little Troll crying. She took him into her room.

"Now, Little Troll, what is all this nonsense?" she said.

"I was cross and I was naughty," sobbed Little Troll.

Little Troll told Mrs Mab what he'd done and he told her about the monster.

"Hmm," said Mrs Mab. "Well, I don't see any monster here now, do you?"

Little Troll looked around the room. He looked on Mrs Mab's desk. He looked under his chair.

"No," he sniffed.

The bell rang for playtime.

"Now, Little Troll," said Mrs Mab. "I think you'd better go back to your class and say sorry to Miss Witherkins."

"Yes, Mrs Mab," said Little Troll.

Little Troll went back to his class.

"Sorry, Miss Witherkins," he said. "I was feeling cross, like a monster."

Miss Witherkins looked at Little Troll for a moment. Then she smiled.

"Actually, Little Troll, I was feeling a little cross too," she said. "Perhaps there's a bug going round – a cross bug."

"Perhaps," agreed Little Troll.

"Well, we'll both have to try and cheer up, won't we?" said Miss Witherkins.

"Yes, Miss Witherkins," said Little Troll.

"Good," said Miss Witherkins. "Now, off you go and play."

Little Troll went outside. He sat on the playground steps.

"Hi, Little Troll!" said Sprite. She sat down next to her friend. "What's the matter?" she asked.

"I was feeling cross," said Little Troll. "I wanted to be a monster and eat you all up."

"Well, I don't think we'd taste
very nice," said Sprite. "Have a
bite of my apple instead." She
offered Little Troll her apple and
he took a bite.

"Thanks," said Little Troll. He
was feeling much happier now.

"Come and play with Elf and
Faun and Goblin and me,"
said Sprite. "It's not the same
without you."

Little Troll smiled. It was his first smile that day. "OK," he said.

Little Troll played tag with Sprite and Elf and Faun and Goblin. He ran and chased and laughed. He had a great time.

And the monster was nowhere to be seen.

LITTLE TROLL LEAVES HOME

Little Troll was bored.

"Why don't you read your comic?"
said his mum.

But Little Troll was bored of
reading his comic.

"Why don't you ride your bike?" said his dad.

But Little Troll was bored of riding his bike.

He watched TV for a bit. But soon he was bored of that too.

"Home's boring," he said. "I'm leaving. I'm going to see the world and have some fun."

So he packed up a few things in his backpack and set out to see the world.

As Little Troll walked, he whistled. He thought about all the interesting things he was going to do.

He thought about all the interesting people he was going to meet.

He thought about all the fun he was going to have.

How glad he was that he was
leaving home!

Little Troll had not gone far
when he came to a field.

In the field, some of his friends were playing football. Sprite was there, and Elf and Faun and Goblin. "Hey, Little Troll!" they called. "Come and play!"

But Little Troll shook his head. "I'm off to see the world," he said. "I'm going to have some fun."

"Well, how about a game of football before you go?" they said.

Little Troll liked playing football. He liked it a lot.

"OK," he said. "Just one quick game, then I'm off."

The football game was fast and furious. First one team scored and then the other. On and on it went. They played for over an hour, until at last Little Troll scored the winning goal.

Little Troll and his friends lay
down to rest in the sunshine.

"Let's go swimming in the river," said Faun. The others agreed.

But Little Troll shook his head. "I'm off to see the world and have some fun," he said.

"A swim will cool you down before you start your journey," said Elf.

Little Troll *was* very hot and he *did* have a long way to go.

"OK," he said. "Just one quick dip, then I'm off."

The water was cool and clear.
The friends splashed and swam
and ducked and dived. They had a
piggy-back fight. They had a
swimming race. Goblin won and
Little Troll came second.

After that the friends flopped on
the riverbank and lay in the sun.
Soon they were hot again.

"Let's go and get ice-lollies," said
Goblin. The others agreed.

But Little Troll shook his head.
"I'm off to see the world and have
some fun," he said.

"You can take an ice-lolly with you," said Elf.

Little Troll *was* hot and he *did* like ice-lollies.

"OK," he said. "I'll just come with you to the shop, then I'm off."

Together the friends went to the ice-lolly shop.

The ice-lollies were lovely and cold. Little Troll's lolly was a space rocket with four different colours.

"Let's eat our lollies at the playground," said Faun.

"Good idea!" agreed Goblin.

"Then we can play for a while."

But Little Troll shook his head. "I'm off to see the world and have some fun," he said.

"Sit down and eat your lolly first," said Sprite.

Little Troll thought for a moment. He could do with a little rest. He liked the playground too.

"OK," he said. "I'll just stay for a bit, then I'm off."

So he went with his friends
to the playground.

At the
playground
there were
lots of
things to
play on.

There was
a big slide and a little slide.

There were
swings and
a roundabout
and a
seesaw.

There was a climbing frame and
a rocket.

There was a giant rope spider's web.

Little Troll had a go on them all.

It was nearly tea-time when,
at last, the friends left the
playground.

"We've got to go home for tea
now," sighed Elf.

"Won't you come with us?" said
Sprite.

"No, no," said Little Troll,
"I'm off to see the world and have
some fun."

Little Troll waved his friends goodbye.

He walked on alone. As he walked, he whistled.

He tried to think about all the
interesting things
he was going
to do.

He tried to think about all the
interesting people he
was going to
meet.

He tried to imagine all the
fun he was going
to have.

But all he could think about
was how much fun he'd just had
and the friends he'd left behind.

He thought about home. He
thought about his mum and dad.
He thought about his friends.

Little Troll's steps got smaller.
His whistling grew fainter...

The road ahead looked very, very long and big and empty. It didn't look much fun.

Little Troll stopped walking. He stood still.

Then he turned and ran back to
join his friends.

"Hi, Little Troll," said Sprite.
"You came back!"

"I thought you were going
to see the world and have fun,"
said Faun.

Little Troll shrugged. "There's no hurry," he said. "I can see the world another day."

"Yes," agreed Elf and Goblin. "Let's go home," said Sprite. So together the friends set off home.

As they walked, they laughed
and talked and sang.

"Actually, you know, home's
quite good fun, isn't it?" said Little
Troll when they were nearly there.
"Maybe I won't leave after all."